Walt Disney's

ALICE in Wonderland

Pictures by the Walt Disney Studio
adapted by AL DEMPSTER from
the motion picture based on the
story by LEWIS CARROLL

GOLDEN PRESS • NEW YORK

ALICE was growing tired, listening to her sister read. Just as her eyes began to close, she saw a white rabbit hurry by, looking at his pocket watch and talking to himself. Alice thought that was very curious indeed—a talking rabbit with a pocket watch! So she followed him into a rabbit hole beneath a big tree.

And down she fell, down to the center of the world, it seemed.

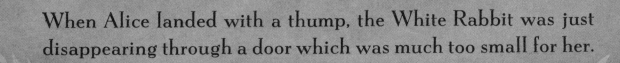

When Alice landed with a thump, the White Rabbit was just
disappearing through a door which was much too small for her.

Alice drank from a bottle on the table and shrank away to a very tiny size. But now she could not reach the key to the little door!

At last Alice found a way to get through the little door. Seated on a bottle, she floated into Wonderland on a mysterious sea.

On the shore of the Wonderland Sea, Alice joined a race. It had
no beginning, it had no end; you just ran around and around.

On through Wonderland Alice went, looking for the White Rabbit. She met two jolly fellows, Tweedle Dum and Dee.

They did not know the Rabbit, but they told Alice a wonderful story of a Walrus and a Carpenter who walked beside a sea.

Alice listened politely. Then she hurried on. And at a neat little house in the woods at last she met the White Rabbit himself!

The Rabbit sent Alice into his little house to hunt for his gloves.
But instead she found some cookies labeled Take One. So she did.

The cookie made Alice grow as big as the house. What a sight!
Rabbit and his friend Dodo thought she was a dreadful monster.

Alice picked a carrot from Rabbit's garden. Eating it made her small again, so small that she was soon lost in a forest of grass.

Soon Alice found herself in a garden of talking live flowers. There were bread-and-butterflies and rocking-horseflies, too.

Alice thought the garden was a pleasant place. But the flowers thought Alice was just a weed, so they would not let her stay.

Next Alice met a haughty Caterpillar blowing smoke rings. He
told Alice to eat his mushroom if she wished to change her size.

Alice sampled one side, and shot up taller than the tree-tops, frightening the birds. But another bite made her just the right size.

"Now which way shall I go?" Alice wondered. The signposts she found along the path were no help—they pointed all over.

"If I were looking for the White Rabbit, I'd ask the Mad Hatter,
said a grinning Cheshire Cat up in a tree. "He lives down there."

Alice found the Mad Hatter and the March Hare celebrating
their un-birthdays at a tea party. She joined them for a while.

After that nonsensical tea party, Alice wanted to go home. But none of the strange creatures she met seemed to know the way.

Alice wandered into the Queen's Garden. But the gardeners could not help her. They were all busy as could be, painting the roses red.

Soon along came the Royal Procession. And who should be the royal trumpeter for the Queen of Hearts but the White Rabbit himself!

The Queen asked Alice to play croquet. But Alice did not like the looks of the game. "Off with her head!" cried the Queen.

Away Alice ran, while the army of cards gave chase, down all the tangled paths of Wonderland, and back to the river bank.

"I'm glad to be back where things are really what they seem,"
said Alice as she woke up from her strange Wonderland dream.